LEMONADE PARADE

Written by Ben Brooks   Illustrated by Bill Slavin

ALBERT WHITMAN & COMPANY
Morton Grove, Illinois

Library of Congress Cataloging-in-Publication Data

Brooks, Ben (Benjamin)
Lemonade parade/Ben Brooks:
illustrated by Bill Slavin.
p. cm.
Summary: When Patty and her friends get
discouraged over lack of business at their
lemonade stand, her father shows up in a series
of outlandish disguises to boost sales.
ISBN 0-8075-4432-9
[1. Moneymaking projects—Fiction.
2. Costume—Fiction.] I. Slavin, Bill, ill.
II. Title.
PZ7.B79125Le 1992   91-34870
[E]—dc20   CIP
                             AC

Published in 1992 by Albert Whitman & Company,
6340 Oakton, Morton Grove, Illinois 60053-2723.
Published by permission of Kids Can Press Ltd.,
Toronto, Ontario Canada.

To my loving parents,
for always supporting my wild imagination
B.B.

To Kathy, Graham, Bridget and Tim
B.S.

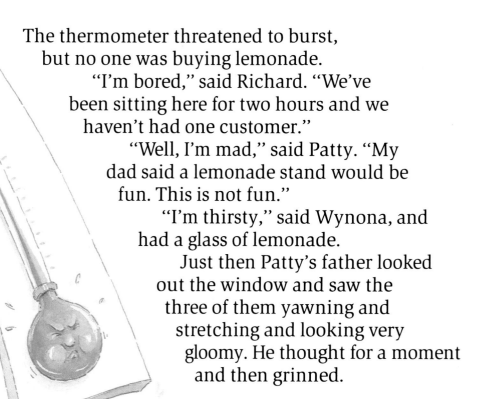

The thermometer threatened to burst,
but no one was buying lemonade.
"I'm bored," said Richard. "We've
been sitting here for two hours and we
haven't had one customer."
"Well, I'm mad," said Patty. "My
dad said a lemonade stand would be
fun. This is not fun."
"I'm thirsty," said Wynona, and
had a glass of lemonade.
Just then Patty's father looked
out the window and saw the
three of them yawning and
stretching and looking very
gloomy. He thought for a moment
and then grinned.

Ten minutes went by. The heat beat down.
"That's it," announced Patty. "I quit."
"Wait," said Richard, pointing down the street.
"Who's that?"
"He sure is big and hairy," said Patty.
"I think he's coming over here," said Richard.
"I want to go swimming," said Wynona.

"Hello there," boomed the man. "After a tough morning shovelling rock and looking for gold, a prospector needs some lemonade."

"Wow!" said Richard. "Our first customer."
"Here you go," said Patty. "Ten cents, please."
"Weird beard," said Wynona.

"Here's a quarter. Keep the change," said the prospector, and drank his lemonade. Then he trudged to the end of the block, around the corner and out of sight.

Patty, Richard and Wynona waited for their next customer. Ten more minutes passed. The heat beat down and the tar oozed up out of the pavement.

"I guess that's it," said Patty.

"I hope you're not closing," said a man wearing a helmet. "I have driven across three continents in my super-fast, custom-built race car, just to get a glass of lemonade."

"Wow!" said Richard. "Our second customer."

Patty quickly poured some lemonade. "Ten cents, please," she said.

The race-car driver took the glass and gulped the lemonade.

"So where's your car?" asked Wynona.

"Ah, that was great! Here's fifty cents. I've won a lot of races this year, so keep the change." With a wave, the race-car driver dashed to the end of the block, around the corner and out of sight.

Patty, Richard and Wynona were amazed. They poured several glasses of lemonade and waited anxiously. The heat beat down, the tar oozed up out of the pavement, and a tired old dog wandered by in search of shade.

They were watching a fly swimming in the lemonade when their next customer bumped into the stand.

"Greetings, fellow earthlings! I have just returned from Venus, Mars, Saturn and Baroonga and I really need some lemonade. Space food packs well, but it tastes like sawdust."

"Wow!" said Richard. "Our third customer."

"You must be really thirsty," said Patty. "Here are two glasses for the price of one."

"Baroonga?" asked Wynona.

"Thank you," said the astronaut, and drained both glasses in a second. "Here's a dollar. Keep the change so you can continue this important service to the galaxy." With that, the astronaut bounced to the end of the block, around the corner and out of sight.

Patty looked up the street for more customers. Wynona looked down the street. No one in sight.

The heat beat down, the tar oozed up from the pavement, the dog snoozed under a shrub, and a caterpillar slunk across the sidewalk. Richard was almost asleep. When someone whispered "Psst!" he fell right off his chair.

"Is this lemonade safe to drink? I'm a top-secret, undercover, double triple agent and it's really hot in this coat."

"Wow!" yelled Richard. "You're a spy!"

"Shh, kid!" whispered the man. "You'll blow my cover."

"Here's your lemonade," whispered Patty, looking both ways before handing him the glass.

"Nice hat," said Wynona. "Patty's mom has one like that, but hers is clean."

"Here's two bucks," said the spy, and drank the lemonade. "Keep the change. And if anyone asks, you never saw me." Without a sound, the spy tiptoed to the end of the block, around the corner and out of sight.

The heat got worse, but business got better. By the end of the day, Patty, Richard and Wynona had sold all their lemonade, and to the most amazing people:

a rock star   and a clown.

A deep-sea diver

and a firefighter.

A retired pirate

and a lion tamer.

A vacuum-cleaner salesman bought
the very last glass.

Patty, Richard and Wynona raced into the house. Patty's father was on the couch, snoring.

"Dad!" shouted Patty. "We made thirteen dollars and eighty-five cents from our lemonade stand!"

"No kidding," he mumbled.

"We could go to the movies," Patty went on.
"And get popcorn."

"We could buy double-scoop, chocolate-dipped, neon-marshmallow ice-cream sundaes with gobs of whipped cream on top!" said Richard.

Patty's dad moaned quietly.

"We could put our money in the bank," said Patty.

"Great idea," said her dad. "Save it for a rainy day."

"Or," said Wynona. "We could buy more lemonade."